SWINTONS GO TO ARUBA
R/S

by
Tracie Walker

North America & international
toll-free: 1 888 232 4444 (USA & Canada)
phone: 250 383 6864 ♦ fax: 812 355 4082

SWINTONS GO TO ARUBA
R/S
WELCOME BACK!!

Narrator: *Couldn't stay away could you? Me either. But it's in my contract. Allow me to re-introduce myself. I'm you're friendly neighborhood storyteller. I've got my own title and everything "Narrator".*

Remember wha' happened? You've got two women, Sasha Swinton and Sizzli Swinton, living two completely opposite lives in separate parts of the world. Only to find out that they are not only sisters, but Royalty. They've even got a tattoo to prove it, the R/S on their left shoulder. Despite their differences, they'll have to work together to find other members of their family who could be anywhere in the world.

With a sneeze, the need for a hug, a little magic and a lot of improvisation, they'll put everything in motion. In the end they'd be a growing family. Better yet –

A PALACE AWAITS. *(I just did that for effect).*

If you know like I know – it won't be easy. And if you didn't read the first part, you wouldn't know. Sooo, I'm here to tell ya. Just try to keep up. These ladies are on the move. They move often – they move fast. Frequent flyer miles? Not quite.

Makes you want to keep reading doesn't it?

Let me break it down fer ya: Sasha and Sizzli, are on their first adventure to find any parts of their long lost family. They'll literally get dropped somewhere in the world, track down a sneeze, run into a family member, locate the R/S on the left shoulder, give them a "hug" and The Strangest Thing - A-chew, (I sneezed) happens. Sounds easy enough. Well that is if they don't hurt each other or get hurt in the process.

I should mention that the first time out, since the two couldn't agree on a location, The Strangest Thing decided for them. Can't wait to see where they end up.

Humm with these girls?

> *Which will come first?*
>
> *Impression? Intention? Payback? Or Just due?*
>
> *I only hope wherever they go,*
>
> *that it's not flu - season.*

OK – the rhyming could use a little work. So lets do this.

SWINTONS GO TO ARUBA
R/S
INDEX

Swintons go to Aruba

R/S

CAST OF CHARACTERS

Narrator	*Somebody's got to tell the story*
Sasha Swinton	Eccentric ex- millionairess who lost her fortune to love
Sizzli Swinton	Every day Jane type who always gets caught up in something
Wilhoit Knubbins	Biological son of Frick & Frack Knubbins
Wilbert Knubbins	Adopted son of Frick & Frack Knubbins
Lytl Guy	Wilhoit's lifelong friend
*Tuff Guy	Lytl's sister
*Big Guy	Lytl's brother
*Tall Guy	Lytl's other brother
Dunno B. It	Collaborator of "IT the mall
Whatabout It	Husband and father of one
Thinabout It	Wife and mother of the same one

Dindu It	Baby of the above two
Knot It	He's the bad seed of the family
Danna Dain	Server at The Plaace 2 B
Mr. Clue	A pretty good boats man himself
The Strangest Thing	**The Hostest with the Mostest**

Better known to the Arubians as "The Destroyers"

Swintons go to Aruba

R/S

SCENE I

GRAVITY – GOTTA LOVE IT

Scene: The girls blinked and their surroundings were different. Great aerial view of the water front though. They could see what looked like two sets of clouds. One set just below them and the other, was it's shadow on the water Lots of sandy beaches. Beautiful blue water and boats in the water. Closer to shore was the most perfectly manicured array of trees and bushes and so many wild flowers with everything in it's place. All this surrounding prime property for development. Consequently, lots of construction going on. At least it looks that way. What's the use in having sand, surf and boats without boat houses and a mini mall for their convenience.

Narrator: *So here we are. They left The Others to find the others. Without thinking, Sasha lost her grip, The Strangest Thing vanished and the land got closer quickly. Goodbye view. The two fell to the ground. No broken bones or anything.*

Anyway, where ever they are, it's totally different from either Sasha's really, really big home or Sizzli's "human roach motel" Question is - where are they now???

Sizzli *(picking herself up and checking knees and elbows)*

Wooowww. What a rush!!! Ahhhh Maaaan! Did you see the view from waaaaay up there!!! Better than a painting by Picosti in watercolor. Never seen anything like it.

Sasha *(pressing down her dress and patting her hair)*

UUHHH! If I **have** to fly, I prefer an airplane. Humpf! I fly allll the time, allll the time. I'll never travel unless it's **First Class.** IIIII get frequent flyer miles, plenty of peanuts and everything. I'd expect that you've never been on a plane. That figures! Humpf!

Nowwww. Where are we? Humpf *(she yells in the air)* **get back here you ... you STICK THING!!!! Humpf!**

Sizzli

It's The Strangest Thing and because you talk so much, I have no idea where we are. What I did hear was that when you loose your grip it, he, whatever would be gone. You lost your grip. You might want to work on that.

Narrator: *She'll get her chance. Hold up — see that sign? Looks like there's a message too.*

Aruba's Coat of Arms has been in use since November 15, 1955.

(Painted at the bottom)

Sasha, GO HOME! We just don't like you!!!

Narrator: *Sasha saw the Country but couldn't quite read the painted part.*

Sasha

Oh wow! We're in Aruba! Humpf *(squinting)* What's that say at the bottom?

Sizzli

Yeah. Aruba. Uhh! They don't like you. *(thinking - I truly understand!)* I wonder why?

Sasha

Oh you're funny. Ha ha! I just love Aruba and they like me plenty. The people are sooooo accommodating. But of course they **have** to be to me. I'm Sasha Swinton. People MOVE when they hear my name. Humpf!

Narrator: *I'll bet they do.*

1

Sasha

We're in Aruuuuba, We're in Aruuuba. Oh the powder white sandy beaches with the worst worry being which one of Aruba's enticing restaurants to eat at.

Narrator: *Yeah. I read the brochure too.*

Sizzli *(shaking her head)*

Sasha, the fact that we really are related is my worst worry.

Sasha

Forget you Sizzli. Sizzli! More like sputter!!! Humpf! AAAHH! Fooood Woo hoo! There's great fish here. Of course – not like the FAAB-U-LUSSS lobsters I'd have brought to me allllll the way from Main and delivered to me personally by the head of the D.O.L.E. that's The Department of Lobster Excavation.... Humpf. Or maybe I'll go snorkeling, I hear the instructor has been flown in allllll the from......

Sizzli *(interupts)*

Girl, I'll put your head under water without the snorkel if you don't shut up. We have a job to do - find our family.

Sasha *(frustrated)*

FIND OUR FAMILY, FIND OUR FAMILY! Humpf! Just 'cause some stupid pogo stick thingy; *it was the strangest thing I've ever seen* -- with a lot of money; *well I **love** that part* ... says that we have to find some -family, *they can't have my share* -- doesn't mean that we really have family all over the world. Royalty schmoyalty. *Ok the palace **really was** impressive.* Humpf!

Tell you what! You go look for family in…HAAAAL. I mean Haltovista! Humpf!!

Sizzli

Unfortunately, *sister dearest*, if it weren't for the fact that we had to be at the same destination, to do this, I'da gone in a totally different direction. You talk too much.

Now please enlighten me. Where in your little world is Haaal-to Vista aaall the way from?

Sasha

Heeere silly! Haltovista, Aruba. It was in the paper. You apparently don't read either. Humpf! I only had the finest reading tutor, flown alllll the way from Switzerland in my very own private jet, and delivered to me personally by the Dean of Learn Good Schools. Humpf!

Narrator: *I knew it! She **read** the brochure.*

Sasha *(cont.)*

We had to do a report about the plague of Haltovista. Infected the majority of the population. I wonder what ever happened to that part of Aruba? Maybe I'll get lucky and you'll be struck by a plague while we're here!! Humpf

Sizzli

I can't see you closing your mouth long enough to read or write and I've already been struck with a plague. Should be – front page news: Plague Sasha! The mouth that keeps **going** and **going** and **going,** for no apparent rational reason what-so-ever!! May cause populus interuptus.

Narrator: *Did she say front page news? I just had a flashback. Wait, popu what?*

Sizzli *(cont.)*

This can't be my life. My life was just fine. *(she yells in the air)* **YOU MIGHT BE STRANGE BUT YOU'RE NOT FUNNY!!**

Sasha

It's The Strangest Thing! Humpf! Come oooonn, WE'RE IN ARUUUUBA!!! *(shimmeying her shoulders)* All this beautiful water and beautiful sandy beaches, and beautiful ME what could be better? Humpf!

Sizzli

Do you want the truth? *(slapping her hand to her four head)* Come on. Let's find some food. There's got to be some place close by to eat, And me, without my Ghost Toasties....

Sasha

Food! Well it's about time. I know exactly where to go. Humpf!

Sizzli

I'll bet you reeeally don't!

Sasha *(cont)*

Waite a minute! Ghost WHAT????

Sizzli *(shaking her head – again)*

Ghost Toasties. You've never heard of Ghost Toasties and evaporated milk? It's just my most favorite breakfast in the whole wide world. Brought allll the way from the grocery store and delivered to my mouth personally by my spoon!

Sasha

Ha - Ha! You just tickle my funny bone. Humpf . I wanna go to the beach. **Nooowww!!!!** I got a swiiiiimsuit, I got a swiiiimsuit. *(then she thought about it)* Oh man, *(she yells)* I must have left my bag with two hands – back – in the limousine! *(shaking her head)* I really wish I could find my bag.

Narrator: *Just as she said that, her left shoulder started to itch so she reached over with her right hand and scratched it. Da da daaaa!*

Sasha *(cont.)*

You think it'll be alright? Humpf! I want my limo….At least we could ride instead of walk. I don't do walking. I'd have my driver take me where ever I wanted to go alllll the time…..alllll the time. Humpf!

Sizzli *(shook her head - again)*

Can it Sash! That TACKY BAG is at The Others and I hope my girl Ganna made it alright in the trash.

Waite a minute! You wouldn't happen to be referring to a grey limo?

Sasha *(says whimpering)*

OOOF Course!!! That's all I had left since that insolent excuse of a driver *(what is his name?)* quit and took my Benz ....Humpf

Narrator: Never could remember his name.

Sizzli *(interrupts)*

That was you! You were that maniac that almost ran me over when I was already late for work! Ugg - I shoulda known. I saw what you said too. **MORON!!!** right back atcha!

Narrator: Sniff! Sniff! Do you smell payback?

Sasha

That was you? Opps! Humpf!

Sizzli

Opps! Opps! I really feel these people. I didn't like you before. Now, I'm liking you less. ---- OPPS!

Narrator: The girls are walking along the beach. Sasha hears a sneeze so her entire body clenches and she looked at Sizzli... remembering what The Strangest Thing said alllll the way from the palace. Yuk yuk.

Sasha

You hear that?

Sizzli *(looking in the other direction)*

Hear what? All I hear is you steady yacking and I'm trying to ignore you.

Narrator: She sticks her neck out with her ear in the direction of the sneeze and heard it again but louder this time.

Sasha

I heard someone sneeze! There it is again! You didn't hear that? It's this way.

Narrator: Sasha grabs hold to Sizzli's arm and took off running in the direction of where she thought she heard the sneeze. Of course it was down the hill on a serious decline from where they stood. Sizzli snatches her arm away and Sasha slips and falls face first. Rolling over and over from the other side of the beach, straight to the one side, past the buildings through the very sandy/dusty construction dirt. I did mention rolling over and over. OOPPS!!!

Sizzli *(running down the hill after her)*

AAAHHH!!!! Sash? You were serious. You really don't do walking. I saw where **that** trip came allll the way from? Talk about a special delivery. AHHH! Welcome to Aruba and thank you for flying --- Sasha!!!

Narrator: I'd give her a 9.9 for the take off and execution. She'll have to come to a stop at some point. Sasha STOOOP! I'm yell-

*ing like she can hear me. OK **now**. She rolls to a stop, stands up, thrusts her head in the air and tries to smooth out her dress.*

Sasha

Thuwie Thuwie. That wasn't funny. Do I look OK? Humpf! Thuwie!

Sizzli

Do you look OK? Actually, you looked almost the same way when I first met you. That's sad. I take it this kind of thing happens to you often. I'll bet you took ballet and your instructor was couriered to you alllll the way from No Balance U. You have scientifically proven that; in this case; the cause and effect of gravity is a beautiful thing. Ha ha ha Don't do walking huh? I see why! Your feet don't like you either. Ha ha ha

I will say that you started off with such enthusiasm; it's the stopping you have a problem with.

Sasha *(yelling)*

Ha Ha Thuwie! Thuwie! I should have run over you... when I had the chance! Humpf! Thuwie!

Sizzli *(snickering).*

It's perfect. You look like an over enthusiastic tourist. Sun and sand! The beach bumbs fashion statement. Good look for you Sash.

OK! There "IT" is. Maybe that's where that sneezes came from..... There's got to be some place to eat. You think you can keep your balance long enough to get some food?

Narrator: *We shall see. What do you know, there IT really is.*

"IT"

What ever it is, that's what we're full of.

Welcome and thanks for stepping in IT.

Narrator: *Sizzli thinks it's probably not a good idea to wipe off so much of the sand. They're at the beach so it can't be that hard to rationalize someone covered in sand, besides Sasha's not that easy to recognize as long as she doesn't say anything. She's also trying to think how they're going to find the sneeze, discretely look for the R/S on the left shoulder of the sneezer, plus explain all the sand to any sane person, without them knowing that Sasha has returned. Right now, the priority is food. At the far end of IT was a restaurant. OH HAPPY DAY!*

Sasha

Look there's a sign on the door. Maybe it's a list of the ingredients in the food. I really hope they've updated their menu. Humpf! At least now you could say that you've eaten more than that Ghosty stuff. Me? I'll have the lobster prepared just the way I remember. Although I'm sure it probably won't be as good as the ones that I get sent to me alllll the way from....

Sizzli *(interrupts)*

Sasha! Sasha! I wish you could just shut up! Not a peep, till we get back to the Palace! Save everybody a headache.

We'll just have to try to blend in. So far nobody knows we're here.

Narrator: *Sizzli's left shoulder started to itch so she reached over with her right hand and scratched it. Don't worry, I won't play the da da daaa thing out.*

*What a predicament. Sizzli's trying to think of something that won't bring out the Arubian arms. This looks more like the makings of Where's Mauldo. Just **don't** guess who's coming to dinner. Am I showing my age here?*

Anyway. Which do you think will come first? Will head to toe sand become the next fashion trend? Will they find food and be able to eat it? Will the person who sneezed have R/S on their shoulder or coincidentally have a cold? Will they find anyone who likes Sasha?

It's said, don't' judge a book by it's cover, lets just hope that Sasha's cover won't be blown --- off.

Swintons go to Aruba

R/S

SCENE II

TWO KNUBBINS AND A LYTL GUY

Scene: At a hut right on the beach front, stood a group of sheds with lockers for the boat supplies and things. Near a group of sheds are two of the finest reasons for being beach bumbs, Wilhoit Knubbins the biological son of Frick & Frack Knubbins and Wilbert, their adopted son who wishes he had a better last name.

Wilbert, wearing cut off shorts, a baggy shirt and sandals. Waxing the surf board thingy that's leaning against the shed. He won't stop until he see's his reflection in the board.

And there at a payphone at the corner of the shops, stood Wilhoit wearing matching cut off shorts, a baggy shirt and sneakers who is supposed to be working on fixing the sail for their boat. It certainly ended up being a short conversation because right after he sneezed, a strange sound got his attention. It was coming from Wilbert's direction and he had to stop that noise.

Narrator: *The fellas, Wilhoit and Wilbert have been sailing partners for as long as they can remember. They're getting ready for:*

"THE WAAAR ON THE WATERRRRRR!!!"

They have it every year and to win The WOW is a sailors greatest honor. The fellas even won last year using a boat, (if you want to call it that) that they found and had to fix from stern to sternum.

It needed a new engine, had holes in the floor boards that needed repair, plus new sails and let's not forget the brakes. Basically they cut and pasted it together. What a project. But after all that hard work, to make it compete able, they pulled off a miracle.

How'd they do it? A lot of hard work, a little bit of faith, a hope and a prayer that The Strangest Thing (ah chew) could happen. Besides, they're a team. Like brothers should be. Isn't the family dynamic a wonderful thing?

Let's get a closer look shall we?

Wilbert *(Looking at his reflection in the board - singing)*

"I'm lookin' at the man in the surfboard, I'm asking him to chaaange his naaame. No message could have been any clearer, If you want to make my life a better place, won't you cut me some slack and just change my naaaame" *(He wrings out the rag and taps his pocket)* I've got rhythm, I've got music, I've got sunshine, who could ask for anything moooooorre. Who could ask – for – annyyythiiinggg – MOOOOOOOORREE! Ha ha.

Narrator: *OK now, wanna know who Wilhoit was on the phone with? His lifelong friend Lytl Guy. Maybe I should mention that not only is his name Lytl Guy, he literally is a little guy. Wilhoit short of, I mean sort of took the little dude under his wing. The thing*

*is, Wilbert doesn't appreciate it when **he** doesn't get all the attention. Actually, he doesn't want any distractions so close to The WOW.
What are friends for? When Wilhoit realized who was making the
noise, he disconnected and went in the direction of the noise.*

Wilhoit

Man, I heard you singin'. Don't do that again. That was baaad.
Baaad I say.

Wilbert

Come on now. I can sing.

Wilhoit

On what planet? You **can** be a painindabutt and you're givin' me
and anybody within earshot a headache.

Take my advice, when you win The WOW, you can go celebrate
some place waaaay off in the faaaarrr distance *(pointing his finger)*
OUTTTT THERE!! Sing your heart out! I'll know where you
are when I hear the dogs barking.

Wilbert

I'll tell you where you can go.

***Narrator:** I don't think he means Haltovista.*

Wilhoit

Come on man. We're almost brothers. - Brother.

Wilbert

Oh brother.

Wilhoit

Yeeeessss. Just call my naaaame and I'll come sailin'!

Wilbert

You're a silly man. I *must* have been dropped on my head sailing with you for so long. Look, you were so busy on the phone, have you got that sail fixed yet? You're lucky I like you. I don't know why my parents adopted you.

Wilhoit

OK so all the good names were already taken from the name pool. Knubbins! Not that I don't appreciate it but look at me. It's because I'm the best sailor you know, you stay around. Plus I'm soooo pretty. Pretty and Knubbins don't match.

Narrator: Well, I've never seen a pretty Knubbins.

Wilhoit (cont.)

The sail's taking a little longer than I thought. I'm working on it!! Somebody put a hole at the bottom and I didn't know where to go for supplies to fix it so close to The Wow. Fortunately, I saw this new shop. He pointed at the sign, which read:

≈ ≈ ≈ ≈ ≈ ≈

Sails-R-Us

Because The Wind Really Blows

≈ ≈ ≈ ≈ ≈ ≈

Narrator: *Yeah - True*

Wilhoit *(cont.)*

While I was at the shop, I saw the Strangest Thing – Ah chew *(he sneezed)*.

Wilbert

Bless you! Did you say you saw a stronger thing? A lock? We've got to get a better lock for the shed?

Wilhoit

No! I said the Strangest Thing - Ah chew *(he sneezed)*.

Wilbert

Bless you. I know. Those new boats are really something strange. Lytl Guy got one for his birthday two years ago. It's totally awesome. It's got an automatic sail retraction system, purrs like a kitten but costs more money, just in upgrades, than either one of us will see in this lifetime. The only reason that I don't step on him is because of his sister.

He may want to learn how to handle such a big ship. If I had such an awesome piece of mechanics on the water, I'd be dangerous. Pretty and Dangerous. Now they go together.

Why do you hang with him anyway? I'm witty! I've got a charming personality!

Wilhoit

You, my nautical friend, are a painindabuttt. *(thinking Why me?)* Man, you just don't know Guy. Actually, he and I graduated from the same school but you wouldn't know that since we adopted you. I heard you've stayed back four times in elementary school and you couldn't sing then either. Guy and I were thick as thieves. Rob from the rich and give -uhh- back.

Wilbert

Trying to be Bobin Kud were ya? You're supposed to rob from the rich and give to the poor and Guy is, by no means, poor. Family's kind of – shall I say – different…What'd he do, rob himself for the insurance?

Narrator: *From out of the corner of his eye, Wilbert sees a gold medallion with R/S in the center and a note underneath. Without being seen Wilbert hurries to pick up the medallion and it shatters but the pieces vanish. He picked up the note and put it in his pocket.*

Wilhoit

Actually, we robbed from other rich people alright. Problem was, most of those people were friends of his father. After we got busted, we literally had to give it back. Haha. Best of buds- Guy and me.

Narrator: *Oh what a coincidence. Just as if he was being called to join the conversation, who should walk up? None other than Lytl*

Guy himself. Great sailor! Has a definite complex about his – self. Wilhoit is short of, I mean sort of the only friend he's got because he doesn't sweat the small stuff. Come on, you know what I mean! It's not his fault that he's height challenged. Short people do have a reason...

Lytl Guy

Hey Hoity. *(turning to Wilbert)* Well, well. If it isn't Bone Head Willy! You should call yourselves Bone Head and Co. Um hum!

Wilbert

Well, well! If it ain't the big guy. It's not your fault you're height challenged

Narrator: *Wait! Didn't I just say that?*

Lytl Guy

That's LYTL GUY. Do I have to spell it out for you? Um hum! Big is my brother.

Wilbert

You mean, you can spell?

Lytl Guy

Yuk yuk! Know what fellas? Not only can I spell, I get great ideas too. It just came to me. You've got a good crew but, so close to The WOW, you could do better. Tell you what. Stop trying to keep fixing that piece of rubble...

Wilhoit (interrupts)

Watch it!!!

Lytl Guy (cont.)

...and get on board The Guys team? Um hum! They say two heads are better than one – what about three?

Wilbert

Are you kidding? Why would I partner with you? I can beat you any day in any weather on any water! On any boat! Why don't you let me sail your boat? It's too big for you anyway.

Narrator: *Maybe he's got a stepping stool. Stranger things could happen.*

Wilhoit

Man Wilbert! Give him a break.*(looking at Guy)* So where are you on your way to?

Lytl Guy

Don't worry about it Hoity my friend. Today is a great day. When I got off the phone with you, I found this medallion. Um hum! It had R/S in the center with a note underneath. When I picked it up, the medallion shattered but the pieces vanished. Go figure! Under it was a note. So of course I picked it up and read it.

Wilbert

Oh! You can read? Will wonders never cease?

Lytl Guy

Shut up Willy! Hoity, keep your friend in check. *(he continued)*

It read:

Responsibilities shift, a change will soon come,
You have traveled the world, but there's work to done.
Look for the others. Not just one party but three,
You'll see that it's more than the place to be.
A Palace awaits

If that's not the sign of a good day, I just don't know what is. So I thought maybe you guys were the others………. Um hum!

Wilbert

Nice story, thanks for sharing, but what's that got to do with us?

Lytl Guy

You don't listen too good. The note says "Look for the others, yadda yadda yadda., so I figured bone head and company must be the parties the note was talking about. Um hum!

Wilbert

You believe in psychic's too?

Lytl Guy

Don't make me get Tough on you bonehead! UM HUM

Narrator: *He really wouldn't want that to happen.*

19

Wilhoit *(interupts)*

It's ok. Please forgive Willie here. I'm trying to get him to see a doctor to change his medication or at least prescribe him some.

Lytl Guy *(frustrated)*

What was I thinking? What would make me believe that we could make any kind of team? Hoity, why don't you let him find another sailing partner? He's got a bad attitude. Um hum.

I'm going to the docs on the other side of Haltovista. I figure my boat would be on safe waters there. I mean who will really look there of all places anyway. Um hum. Wanna go? You need a mental break from…this brain strain. Um hum. I wish he would just go away. Maybe run into the other Guys. That'll learn ya - dern ya.

Narrator: Just then his left shoulder started to itch. He reached over with his right hand and scratched.

Wilbert

Well that's just grand. Put a boat where a plague used to be. Is there even water there? Ha ha. I won't ask how you even had the courage to look where there was so much devastation. And that was a major health risk even BEFORE you showed your little mugg. Or maybe you were the plague all by yourself.

Wilhoit

All right Willie. That's quite enough. *(looking at Guy)* Sure Guy! I wanna get a good look at the upgrades on your boat anyway.

Narrator: *And they started walking away from the shed, towards the side where Guy's boat was docked.*

Lytl Guy *(shaking his head while walking away)*

Why is he like that? What a Pianindabutt! Don't make me call Tuff. Um hum.

Narrator: *Wilhoit and Lytl walked about a block and a half. When Hoity turned around, he didn't see Wilbert. OK - where's Wilbert? He shrugged his shoulders and continued the conversation.*

Wilhoit

You mean **be** tough.

Lytl Guy

No I really mean **call** Tuff. My sister. She's a 6th degree black belt in Mo Duc Soup. She lifts 1000 lbs every three hours. Heck. Last year when she said she was picking up and moving down the street, she literally picked up her house, furniture and all, took it down the street and **dropped it**. Um hum.

Narrator: *Never mind the house she dropped it on. Can you get insurance for that?*

Lytl Guy *(cont.)*

You know what? I think you should join my crew. We can work another strategy for The WOW. Um hum. I wonder if Willie would change his mind. We're running out to time.

Wilhoit

He'll come around. I was telling Willie about the time when you and I did the Bobin Kud thing. Ha ha. Remember that? Oh man we've really seen some things haven't we? Maybe he'll think about the advantages of competing on your boat. We'll have to navigate around being on "the Guy" team. You know how he is.

Actually, you and he have a lot in common. You both been adopted, sailing all your lives and lovin' it and you both can't sing a lick.

The Strangest Thing - Ah chew *(he sneezed)* said you both will be a pintindabutt – all my life. *(he looks up in the air and yells)* **WHY ME!!!**

Narrator: *Maybe it's you're wit and charming personality.*

Lytl Guy

Bless you. Hoity, I think you're tired. You said the strangest thing **said**. Didn't you mean, the strangest thing **is**? Um hum. And I don't give you as much grief as that fruit cake of a relative of yours.

Wilhoit

I happen to like fruit cake. I did mean The Strangest Thing - Ah chew *(he sneezed)* **said**, and really, that's its name. All my years here on the water, I've never seen anything like it. Come on I'll introduce you.

Lytl Guy

It's name? Introduce? It has a name **and** talks? Oh poor Hoity. *(he reaches up and puts the back of his had on Hoity's forehead)* My brother Bright's a psychologist. I'll take you to him. Um hum!

Wilhoit

No really. Guy we've known each other most all our lives. Have I ever lied to you?

Lytl Guy

Lied? Not exactly. I don't know what you call it. Remember when you said that Mr. Ruffin said that we could swim in his pond and YOU told me to go on in you didn't want to get your shoes wet. It was soooo hot that day and I was so ready to swim.....Not only did I step in and get attacked by leaches but the way Mr. Ruffin was shaking that flash light and yellin' "Get off my property. Let's see how fast your little hind parts can run." Um hum. That wasn't funny.

Narrator: That wasn't a flash light either.

Wilhoit

It was only a couple of leaches you wimp, and one - on your big toe. Let's see. Swim trunks -$5.00. Bus to Mr. Ruffins pond - $.75. Removal and medication for the leach on your toe - $.25 co-pay. The look on your face while you ran from Mr. Ruffin - priceless. What's not funny 'bout that?

But really, in all my years here on the water, this was truly The Strangest Thing - Ah chew *(he sneezed)* I've ever seen. He said it's name is The Strangest Thing - Ah chew (*he sneezed*).

Lytl Guy

Oh poor Hoity, I'll take you to see my doctor. You're imagining things and have a cold. This sea air never got to me like this….

Wilhoit

I must be getting a cold or something….. Come on, I'll bet it's at the docs waiting.

Narrator: *Now here we go. Does Lytl ever get a team together before The WOW or even meet the height requirement for the competition? Meanwhile who are the others? Will he realize that he's royalty and perhaps tall enough to see eye to eye with The Strangest Thing? Will Wilbert join the "Guy" team? What ever happened to Wilbert anyway? Is Sizzli still running? Wait - is that a Kite?*

So many questions, so little time.

Swintons go to Aruba

R/S

SCENE IV

THAT'S REALLY "IT"

Scene: The ladies have successfully rolled right past the other side of the beach to the one side, without anyone really paying much attention since this is, after all, a celebration.

The mall was a collaborative effort of the It Family and is under serious construction. You'd be surprised at the kinds of things that are goin' up. That's a good thing isn't it?

At the end of the building of "IT" was a restaurant. Near the front door to the restaurant, looking out the glass was, husband and father of one, Watabout. At the cash register was his charming wife. A woman who some times repeats herself and mother of the same one, Thynabout and lying in the crib, son of the above two, baby Dindu makes three.

Narrator: *I should warn you that Watabout is a great man but he has no teeth plus he's got a lisp. Not a pretty picture! He and his brother Dunno put IT all together for their names sake.*

Let me tell you about Dunno B. It. Good ol' Dunno has three auditors for each store to make sure that he's getting his just due. Calling him a tightwad? He's worse than that Holiday guy.

I guess I should mention Knott. He's the bad seed of the family. Every families got at least one. You know the one who always comes up with the most creative ideas to become an overnight success. At least Knot does have some regular income. He's the Sanitation Coordinator for all of IT and the neighboring shops.

Watabout

Thyna? Do you thee what I thee coming right for uth? All covered in thand. Thith muth be the work of that "find a new gimmic – whatever works" Knot. Alwayth looking to make money.

Thynabout

Not a good idea. Not good. Sand everywhere. Sand everywhere. You can never get it rid of it. *(Looking down at Dindu)* That's my gooooood boy. My goooood boy. *(Tickling under his neck)* OK puddenny. Loooook at you. Looook at you.

Watabout

What ith thith world coming to when gimmiths are taking over, they'll try juth about anything. Head to toe Thand! Won't work! What a meth! And who's gotta clean it up? Me? Uh uh! **KNOT!**

Thynabout

It must be these young people. They always want to come up with something new for The WOW festival. Whatever makes money. Whatever makes money. Well, we **are** on the beach. We are. It may stick to tourists – like those ladies.

Watabout

That's an under thatement

Narrator: *Let's just call it camouflage.*

Thynabout *(squinting her eyes)*

One of them kinda looks familiar. Kinda. Please don't be that woman. She talked entirely too much. **ENTIRELY** too much!

Baby Dindu

WAAAA!! DAAAA! PFFFF! THHHH!

Narrator: *Unfortunately, that's about all babies can verbalize, but it does kinda make sense. If I were a baby, I'd probably want to know - what daaa too. Although the drewling? Like father, like son. Let's hope he grows out of that part.*

Sizzli *(reading the sign out loud)*

"Just Eat It"

Give your mouth something to do.

Rest Rooms ->

Sizzli

Ha! That's cute. In your case, give your mouth something BETTER to do! I hope you chew with your mouth closed.

Narrator: *Sizzli pushes open the door to the shop. It was one of those stores with a cowbell at the top. When she heard it – to her it meant –ON YOUR MARK, GET SET....!!!*

Sizzli *(thinking - this better work.)*

Hi Mr.! Ha ha ha   Nice Store! Can I get a two turkey on wheat please? We're looking for the comedy club, Funny Bones. AAAHH Ha ha! We were told that it was right in this block.

Narrator: *She pulls up close on Whatabout trying to check his left shoulder - nothing*

Whatabout *(thinking)*

Is thith how people where she'th from act in public. Young lady, what is your problem?

Sizzli (cont.)

My girl here is a comedian. AHH MAANN Whuuu!!! We're going to the auditions. She has been practicing her act on me and I just can't get her to stop. You ought to hear her. Go on girl. *(moving towards a booth)* Tell 'um a joke.

Watabout *(not wanting these sandy women in his shop)*

Don't move!! I'll get your thandwiches and thince you are firth time patrons, the desert of the week, justh dew, is free. Now, you thtay here. I don't need my thtore full of thand. Be right back. **Don' move!**

Narrator: *Before, Whatabout went to make the sandwiches, he went to his office to call his brother Dunno to tell him the sand wasn't his fault. Sizzli looks at Sasha all covered in it, hoping that she would change her voice or something. She had no idea what to expect.*

Sizzli *(shacking Sasha)*

Go on girl, tell this lady which came first – ha ha with that voice-you know - that was soooo funny. Come on Ms. Funny Lady. You were on a role a minute ago. Couldn't get you to shut up.

Narrator: *She steps up close to the register, leans behind Thynabout, moves the strap on her left shoulder – again nothing. Sizzli looked up. You could see Sasha open her mouth, take a deep breath but... nothing came out. Not a peep.*

Eyes popping out of her face. Flailing her arms like she should be in a straight jacket, you could see her jumping up and down with her hair standing on end like it's on fire. Mouthing words in what looked like languages that Sizzli wouldn't know anyway. And Thinabout had no idea what was going on. She got as close to the baby as possible. Sizzli is dyin' laughing. – MEDIC!!

Sizzli *(whispers in Sasha's ear)*

Go head Ms. Funny Lady. **You're on a roll - again.** WHUU HUU!

Narrator: *Look at the baby. Do you see the baby?*

Baby Dindu *(thinking)*

I wonder if all big people act like this. How disappointing!

Thynabout

Well now. Lookadair lookadair. My sweet little Dindu. My sweet little Dindu. So she picks him up to pat him on the back.

Narrator: Of course Sizzli leans in to take a look at the babies left shoulder – nothing. I should mention that it smells like the baby needs some attention.

Sizzli *(cathing a wiff and quickly leans back)*

Cute baby.

Tynabout

You must be new in town. You must be. I see Dindu laughing at your friend. We are the "It's". That was my husband Whatabout, I'm Thynabout and this sweet baby is Dindu. Who's not smelling so sweet right now. He really isn't smelling sweet right now.

Narrator: I know right now, she's thanking Dindu for making this crazy woman step back.

Thynabout (cont.)

I never heard of a Funny Bones. Never heard of a Funny Bones. That might be that new thing they's building. Bringin' a lot of new folks around. A lot of new folks.

Sizzli

No I'm sure it's Funny Bones. I've heard that you can get discovered there. *(pointing at Sasha)* She's a star in her own right. Her future could be in your hands.

Narrator: In more ways than one.

Thynabout

I though brother Dunno was working on that. To expand the mall, He's sayin', Laugh At It, not Funny Bones. I think at the other side there's a Funny Bones. A Funny Bones on the other side. This is the one side of the docs. You need to get to the other side.

Sizzli

Other side of the docs? I think we may have rolled right past there. *(snicker)* I want to make sure we're in the place to be for her to get what she deserves.

Narrator: Just due is comming.

Thynabout

Right now it looks to me that she'll do just fine. She'll do just fine. If she can get baby Dindo to smile, she may be on a roll.

Narrator: Been there. Done that.

Sizzli

What we need right now is some food. Do we get a discount if we say the name of the restaurant? When she gets her big break, I'll send a shout out. Ha ha

Narrator: Well so far so good but Sasha is really goin' through some things. If that's sign language I may never learn.

Thynabout

The other side. *(pointing her finger)* I'll bet that's where you'll find your Funny Bones. The other side. All those people are different so you two should fit right in. I think your friend will do just fine. She's practicing so hard, she just might hurt herself. She just might.

Whatabout *(returns with the sandwiches)*

You look a meth. Both of you need baths and thome clothes!! Making a meth in my thtore. I don't know you and I don't like you. (pointing at Sasha) and I definitely don't like you. Makin' a meth all in my thtore. Now **GET OUT!!! NO thanths for thstepping in It.**

Narrator: Now if that's not bad enough, guess who's coming? You can say it. Looks like he's really not having a good day. Actually he's never having a good day.

Dunno

WHAAA DAAA!!!

Narrator: *Sooo that's where the baby got it from. Children really do imitate what they see.*

Dunno *(cont.)*

WHO ARE YOU??? WHAT'S THIS??? LOOK WHAT YOU'VE DONE? LOOOOK AT THIS MESS!!!

Narrator: *He tries to calm down and access the damages. Well that may be what he wants us to think. Actually, he's mad because this has taken him away from his other business. The one that I'm not really supposed to talk about. Something to do with cards and chips.*

Whatabout

OK. What took you tho long? Do you thee thith? I kepp 'em for athh long athh I could. I thaid they'd get their juth dew for free so don't take that out of my rent you....you....

Dunno

STOP talking!!! *(looking at the ladies)* I was meeting my bookie, - I mean accountant and we were talking about who I could cut – I mean where I could make some adjustments... I get a call from one of my spies, - I mean "It-ers", something about two women. One covered in sand – from head to toe, making a mess allllll on my property. You could have gone to either side. Why this side of the docs? *(He takes a closer look...)* Oh wait a minute, I know you?

Narrator: *Well, remember the sound of the cow bell? From the look on Dunno's face, it doesn't mean "thanks for stepping in It". Although they truly have stepped in it. Sizzli's on her mark - sheeez* *set, NOW ---- She grabs Sasha, with one hand and the sandwich bag with the other - looking at Dunno*

Sizzli *(thinking - Oh Snap! Not good)*

Nice meeting you!

Narrator: *Talk about getting a grasp on reality. Sizzli has the sandwich bag in her mouth and.. GOOO !! Out the door she had business, pulling Sasha out the door hitting her head on the cowbell DING!!! and they're off. Stronger than I thought. Up in the air Sasha goes like a Sasha kite, snatching whatever clothes off the racks on her way up. Sizzli's dodging people, and their bags, with Sasha hanging on for dear life.*

Sizzli

Hey Sash. All of these people. All this stuff. You get the award for the tackiest bag ever! ha ha. UHHH – What? What's that you say? I can't hear you! HA!

Dunno *(chasing the sisters all through It.)*

I know that's you Sasha Swinton!! You must not read good!

Narrator: *Not to hear her tell it.*

Dunno *(cont.)*

None of us liked you then and we **still** don't like you. *(shaking his fist)* MORE!!!

Narrator: *Well only half way through It, he stopped running.*

Caught his breath and thought he'd go and start making some phone calls.....

Dunno should have renewed his membership at It's Just X'erSyze. Remember the coat of arms? Now where do the It's keep their armies? In their sleevies or course. Dunno's calling them out -all six of them. His, Whatabout and even Knot. It's their job, no their duty to track down, Sasha Swinton. It can't be that hard since all they have to do is follow the sand or the kite. Let's hope there's a reward. Dunno will need it since clean up ain't cheep. Knot may be his brother but work is money and money is a good thing.

Scene: Back at the restaurant

Thynabout

Now Whatty! Don't let those women disturb your nerves with all that sand. I told the ladies to go to the other side. Go to the other side. Maybe that's where Funny Bones is. I really don't think she was so funny. I really don't.

The one lady was nice but kiiiinda creepy though. Kiiinda creepy. She kept looking to see if something was up our sleeves. What was that about? What? That sandy lady! She didn't say a word. Not a word. Maybe she should stop practicing, clean up and see her doctor. Wait a minute - they didn't pay! They didn't pay!

Whatabout

Don't worry about it. Whoth gonna pay for the clean up? Dunno! Knot! Whoever. He'll have to thpend his money. **Tightwad.** He'll probably contract "IT Thucks" to vacuum thith thtuff up. A comedian twying to audithion! Yeah thure!

35

Narrator: *Hummm!*

Baby Dindu *(thinking)*

(Yeeep. This is what I have to look forward to? I knew I should have read the fine print. I shoulda stayed where I was. It was warm and quiet and dry. I'm not!!! I wasn't smiling? Something's wrong with my bottom. What is that smell??)

WAAAA!! THHHHH!!

Narrator: *I guess Dindu It - did do it. Well maybe It Sucks will get rich from the cleanup if Dunno ever pays! They'll follow the sand to the ladies and send them home, which is what's supposed to happen isn't it?*

Oh right, The ladies didn't locate a sneeze and nobody has an R/S on their shoulders. I'll hope they'll have better luck when they slow themselves down. Lets hope they can stay in one piece. That's family working together don't you think?

Swintons go to Aruba

R/S

SCENE V

SHUDDA MADE A RIGHT

Scene: Now Guy and Hoiti have walked away. There's Wilbert with the rag in one hand, still rubbing his surf board thingy. Talking (to his self but he doesn't know that yet) about Guy finding a medallion with R/S in the center and a note that talks about three parties and he's telling him that because....

Wilbert *(saying sarcastically)*

"That's quite enough". Yeah right. It's never enough unless you're talking about how much fabric it takes to make your boy Lytl a pair of pants. Ha ha Do you get a discount on clothes Guy?

Narrator: *He turned and starts to look around... He's not at the hut anymore. Surprise, surprise Hey Willie! Does something look different to you? OH SNAP, he drops the rag, and takes off running like a maniac – screaming,* **HOITY! HOITY!**

Wilbert *(running really, really fast)*

Where am I? OK somebody's got jokes! This is sabotage if I've ever seen it. First Guy say's he found some medallion. He must have seen me or his spies saw me or something. Then he said that he reads this note that says a palace awaits. - Palace, yeah right. I got a note but it's in my pocket so how'd he know what it said? I look away for a minute - what happened? **Where – am – I**? *Willhoit!!!*

Narrator: OK. *So he's flying. Didn't your mother tell you not to run? He makes the left at the corner running right past the sign:*

HALTOVISTA   *Who knew!*

Maybe - just maybe, he should have hooked a right. He runs smack into the one person that he really doesn't want to see right now. No it's not Sasha. Guess again! It's Lytl's sister - Tuff. Opps!

Wilbert *(cont.)*

Hoity!!! Come back!! I can learn to sing. UUUMMPPFF!!!

Tuff *(looking mean)*
HAAAY!! LOOK WHERE YOU'RE GOING, CHUMP!

Narrator: *Not only did he just bounce off of Tuff like a rubber ball but there's the other brothers Big and Tall.*

I think I should warn you, the Guys might be Big, Tall and Tuff but they all have one thing in common with a door knob. You say boat and they think goat and have this strange craving for milk. So here we go.

Wilbert *(really really scared)*

UUUHH! Hey T. Heard you got a movers job. Congratulations girl. UUUHH Did I wrinkle you? **NO!** Not wrinkle you. I mean wrinkle your shirt! I'll iron it on you. **NO!** I won't iron it on you, uhh - ha. I'll iron it for you. You just take it off – **PLEASE NO!** Not now. If you want me to pick it up later! *(in a whimper)* **PLEASE DON'T HURT ME!!**

Tuff

Well! Well! Look 'a here fellas, if it isn't Wimpbert. I see you runin'. Aren't you a little.L L L....not where you usually are? Hey guys, am I feeling generous today?

Narrator: *I think he meant lost.*

Tall

Gener what?

Tuff

Us - Gener-us

Big

What's this got to do with us? What do we do with the wimp? Let me squash him.

Narrator: *Will Willy cry like a baby or do something else like a baby?*

Wilbert *(hoping he doesn't get pounded)*

HEEEYY Big Guy. You losin' weight? I almost didn't see you. **PLEASE DON'T SQUASH ME.** Squash is a vegetable and you really like vegetables. That's me. Just woooone lonely vegetable **plus aaahhh** it's not dinner time yet? Didn't your mommy tell you to wait for dinner so you could make a happy plate? I know mine did. Happy! Happy! Happy!

Big

Mama said - at dinner time. I have to eat all my vege…vege…

Tuff *(interjects)*

Tables – it's vege-tables!

Tall *(spinning around)*

Turn'n tables. Turn'n tables. I'm getting dizzy.

Narrator: Wait a minute!

Wilbert *(mumbles - Now what?)*

I really wish you Guys, uh I mean, Lady and Messers Guy would just play nice – nice and *(squinting)* not pummel me.

Narrator: Then his left shoulder started to itch so he reached over with his right hand and scratched. He looks up at the group better known to the Arubians as The Destroyers. Tall gets really close and leans down which takes a minute and he grabs Wilbert by the shoulders and Willly's shaking like a dried up leaf on a windy fall day that's just about to drop from the tree.

Wilbert *(still squinting)*

I'm sorry for everything I EVER did - EVER. I'll learn how to sing, IIII prooooomise.

Narrator: *Tall found himself a new squishy toy. He squeezed Wilbert's shoulders like he was checking a loaf of bread.*

Tall

Everybody is so little. *(then he starts singing – badly)* Short people got…uuummm, wait a minute! Short people got…uuummmm, oh I know this one. uuummm. What do short people got?

Big

Ummm! Ummm! Ummm! That feels funny to my mouth. Makes a funny noise. Ummm!

Tuff *(looking up at Tall)*

Short people got rained on last. Now put him down! *(turning to Wilbert)* Looky here little buddy, I could squash you myself but I'm not hungry. Plus, you could get hurt. What made you come from one side to Haltovista anyway?

Wilbert *(completely shocked)*

Haltovista! Oh my!

Narrator: *Told ya. Should have made a right. Now you have to act like you knew tha - you're alright and think how to make a hasty exit out of Haltovista.*

Wilbert *(saying under his breath)*

I read about a plague. It didn't say the Destroyers took over. Same dif I guess.

Well – thanks - Tuff… You to Big - Tall. I'm looking for your brother Lytl. He's with Hoity. You guys seen 'um?

Big

Ummm! Ummm! Ummm!

Tuff *(looking at Big)*

Stop that! Go on Willie!

Wilbert

They were just there with me. I think maybe Guy and Hoity are going to the water to his brand new boat with the retractable sail that purrs like a kitten. Now it's so close to the WOW… I've got to find them. My sail's not fixed. Besides, he's got the best compete able boat. Even wanted me to join his team. I've thought about it. He was saying something about two parties and a palace….

Narrator: *You talk too much Willie!*

Tall

I wonder if ol' Bessie came back. Sure am thirsty

Tuff *(thinking)*

(Palace? Did he just say Palace? I'd like to go to a palace.)

He told me the same thing. He told me to find you and bring you to him. You know?

Big

No he didn't!

Tall *(elbows him in the side)*

If little Willie's our pal. Who's – "**you know**"?

Narrator: *Told you. Door knob.*

Tuff

Excuse me Wimpbert while I have a word with my brothers. *(he pulled them into a huddle)* Hey guys, did you hear what he said? Two parties and a **PALACE**. You know what that means?

Tall

I won't have to duck to get in the door way.

Tuff *(shaking her head)*

No fool! **Money.** Lots and lots of money. Now shut up and let's just follow him. When he finds Lytl and Hoity, we'll get what we deserve.

Big

Desert is good. I like pie!

Tall

He said DESEVRE. Now wait a minute. How are we going to get lots and lots of money when we don't even know which party they're at?

Narrator: *Who invited them anyway?*

Tuff

We'll just have to make sure that he doesn't make a move without us. *(turns back to Willy)*You're in luck. You just so happen to be in our stomping grounds.

Narrator: *Should we take that literally?*

Tuff *(continues)*

We're in the other side. And you were right. The docs. How bout if we escort you. Something could happen to ya. Just want to makes sure that you're safe.

Big

Yeah safe. Safe in baseball, safe in banks, safe driving. Safe is good!

Narrator: *Wilbert's thinking this is not really happening but it could be worse. There's got to be a way to get away – with all his bodily functions - functioning.*

Wilbert

(Oh snap) OK Guys! Messers Guy's! People! You know what? Wait right here. Don't move. I'll be right back.

Narrator: *Slowly I turn. Step by step… You know the rest… OK, what ta do now? He finds a bathroom and steps in. (If you wrote this you'd put a bathroom there too wouldn't you?)*

Wilbert

Wait a minute! The note! Almost forgot. He takes it out of his pocket.

It reads:

Responsibilities shift, a change will soon come,
You have traveled the world, but there's work to done.
Look for the others. Not just one party but three,
You'll see that it's more than the place to be.
A Palace awaits

OK. There's that palace thing again. Maybe Guy wasn't kidding. So now I've got to loose the death squad. Since I'm here what do you know, a potty. I'm not wearing dippies, sooooo…..

Narrator: OK maybe that was too much information. So, when he was done and washed his hands, he looked out the bathroom door and the Guys were still there laughing. Big was still uuummmming, Tall is still asking about a party and Tuff reaches around and smacks both in the back of the head so he turned to the right started walking slowly - again, which got farther and farther until they couldn't possibly see him anymore. Then he took off running. – FAST!! This time, he hooked that right and down the street he had business. At least he's still in one piece. You can see the smoke coming from his shoes though. The stores and people flying past. Actually, he's the one flying. He looks up in the distance and sees banners and balloons and the weirdest kite.

Wilbert

Look at all the preparations for The WOW. That kite may win for originality. It looks so human. OH well, Maybe I should pick up something for my mother to thank her for making me eat my vegetables at dinner time.

Narrator: It would do a mother proud to know that your child listens and applies himself. Big, Tall and Tuff are still wondering where this party is. Outside of one of the little vacant stores was an especially interesting bag. A bag with two hands. Go figure! So he grabbed it up.

Wilbert

This is interesting. Actually it's sort of creepy. You've got to be kidding. I wonder why it has two hands. Well, it's mine now. I wonder what it's worth?

Narrator: Yes he's still running. I know what it's worth and who it belongs to…Now with bag in arm, he at least knows that he's on *the other side. He's never been through Haltovista. Now he can say he's been to Haltovista and survived. From the path he's on, he sees a building.*

Wilbert

Great, I don't think the Guy's saw which way I went. *(looking at the building)* Nice! I need a place to catch my breath and lay low for a minute and this looks like the place for me.

It's daytime, why is the building all lit up. Whats that about?

Narrator: *At a closer look, over the awning it reads The Plaace 2 B. Go Figure! We may see some familiar faces here. Wilbert hears this loud rumbling. There's no construction going on so that's not it. I know! He hasn't had anything to eat all day. FOOD. It was his stomach. He looks inside and sees a very large lady who must be the Hostess standing behind this huge salad/pasta bar with her hand on her waist.*

Wilbert

I didn't know that they were building another restaurant over here Looook at that buffet and salad bar. That lady standing there looks hungry. Just let me have some pasta while I hide from the Guys.

Swiintons go to Aruba

R/S

SCENE VII

THE PLAACE 2 B

Scene: Sizzli's running zigging and zagging, past the docs to the other side trying to loose Dunno and not loose Sasha in the process who's holding on for dear life. Thinking what would possibly make all of Aruba not want Sasha around?

Just ahead she sees a tall bright light surrounding a building. On the awning to the building reads "The Plaace 2 B". The inside looked very well put together. Marble flooring, crystal chandeliers, real oak chairs, silk clothes on the tables even a salad/pasta bar at the back with a mini bar for their convenience A perfect hiding place.

So we're in another conundrum. Which will come first? Just due, dajavu or the simple taming of the shrew that's flying through the air?

Narrator: *The best part - Sasha's voice has left the building.*

Sizzli

Hey Sash. The sign says, The Plaace 2 B. I know you can read but I just wanted to VERRRBALIZE it fer ya. Ha! It's day time. I wonder why they have so many lights on? I'd hate to see their electric bill.

Narrator: Sasha's just a little bit bitter. She could say whatever, in any language but weee can't heear you. Ha! With some practice, she might get the landing on point but just not this time. OOOHHH! Sheeez down. That's gotta hurt. Sheez up. Sheez good.

Sasha *(pressing down her dress and patting her hair and mumbles)*

Thew thewie HUMPF. I HAVE NEVER...IN ALLLL MY LIFE.....HUMPF! That was embarrassing, humiliating, un called for, un civilized, and over all not nice ...humpf!

Sizzli *(catching her breath)*

Just so you know, this - by no means counts as frequent flyer miles and those weren't peanuts.

Narrator: Maybe she'll learn to keep her mouth shut.

Sasha *(signaling as best she can)*

(Looks around and shrugging her shoulders) -Where are we? *(Pointing to the bag, chomping repeatedly)* - Sandwich! *(Looks around again rubbing her hands together with a smirk)* – Nice place!

Sizzli *(as if totally understanding)*

Lady, you're heavy! I'm glad I didn't have to carry your un balanced butt. Like I said, we're in The Plaace 2 B. Yeah, it's a nice place. See that table waaaay over there by the salad/pasta bar? Go to that table and cop a squat. Here! Take your sandwich. Give your mouth something constructive to do and don't say a word. That's right. You can't. Ha ha.

Sasha *(mouthing)*

HA HA Humpf!

Sizzli

Aren't you glad you didn't loose your grip this time? You could still be alllll the way on the one side panicking allll by yourself with no body to not talk to. That would be a shame! Haaa

How did we get from mouth that keeps going to silence is golden? Which by the way, is a gift. *(singing)* Who could ask for anything moooooore! .

Narrator: *OK that's not nice.*

Sizzli *(cont.)*

Let me think. We were in front of the restaurant, you wouldn't shut up. I wished you would, my shoulder itched, I scratched and the next thing, I know, not a wooord from ya. I may learn to like this R/S thingy.

Sasha *(rubs her left shoulder and shrugs)*

Sizzli

I wonder what that's all about? I'll have to ask The Strangest Thing when I see him. Didn't you make a wish too?

Sasha *(nodding and signing the best she can)*

Yep!! Extends her hands like big and makes like she putting a bag on her shoulder.

Sizzli

OH NO! Not that **tacky** bag....

Narrator: *Sasha starts walking towards the salad/pasta bar, takes a bite of her sandwich and scans the room. Well at the other end of the room sitting at a table, in the corner, was a tired Wilbert with this tacky bag with two hands at his feet trying to open it but that just wasn't working. Behind the buffet was Danna Dain, the Hostess. Kinda favors Sizzli's best friend in the whole wide world.*

Sasha's hair stood straight up on her head, her mouth got wide enough to fit the entire building, and her eyes got as wide as saucers. Not really a pretty picture.

Sasha

(shaking Sizzli's whole body, pointing to the other side of the room...)

Sizzli *(looking where Sasha is pointing.)*

What Sash! What's up with this grabby shaky thing? Oh snap. That can't be the....the.....

Narrator: *BAG!!! And yea' it's still tacky.*

Sasha

(Jumping up and down, clapping her hands and took off towards Wilbert).

Narrator: *I don't think Wilbert was really ready for this. Not some lady all covered in dirt or something flapping her arms and waiving her hands like she's about to take off and her mouth moving in languages that he wouldn't understand anyway...zooming past Danna Dain. She didn't look like that when she was Sasha kite or maybe she did. I wasn't looking up.*

Wilbert *(looking shocked)*

Why is that maniac coming towards me? STOOOOP!!! *(He extended his arms and braces himself before she knocks them both down.)*

Narrator: *You think Wilbert's getting this strange feeling of da-javu? Sizzli's right on her tail. Kites? Tails? Get it?*

Sasha *(Off the chest of Wilbert she bounced)*

UMPF!!

Sizzli *(sarcastically)*

Girl! You don't do walking. You aren't good on the ground at all. Stopping obviously doesn't quite werk fer ya either.

Narrator: *She IS better in the air.*

Sizzli *(looking at Wilbert)*

Hey mister. You alright?

Wilbert *(pulling himself together)*

Look, lady, I'm tired. Don't tell me you know "The Guys". Alright, I'll take them to the party. What???

Sasha *(pointing and mouthing)*

That's my bag!!!. humpf

Narrator: *She sees that it's now heavier than before. It belongs to her so it had to grab a few things. But wait a minute! Look at the bag! You thought it was a misprint about the bag with two hands? NOOOOO! It literally has two hands and puts them up as if to give Sasha a hug. Isn't that cute? She picks up the bag by both hands or handles - whichever and swings it from left to right singing...very very quietly I might add....*

Sasha

Aaaand to the left side. Theeen to the right side. Aaaand to the left side. Theeen to the right side. Humpf. *(patting it)* Oh my precious. I've missed you. Where have you been? I know you've picked up soooo many absolutely incredible things from soooo many incredible places just to deliver them to me. Please let me see that you've picked up some aspirin. Humpf

Narrator: *She puts it down and starts pulling out stuff, like the mad woman she is, looking for anything to relieve her headache. If you remember that bag, out of the it comes a mixer, a helmet, mop, glasses, shoes, a lamp, wigs, a bag of nails; both metal and finger, a hair dryer, an iron, an air tank, keys, a spare tire, a bubble gum machine, some paper and pen, and finally another dress. Look ma, no aspirin.*

Sizzli

I thought we got rid of that tacky thing. Now I've got a plague with a tacky HAND bag. **Sasha Swinton, you can never, in life, make another wish!!!** Why didn't I see the hands before?

Sasha *(Grabs the paper and pen and starts to write)*

Didn't C cause your STUUU *(and the pen ran out).*

Narrator: *What??? She must still be hungry.*

Sizzli

Being with you all this time, has it ever plucked you in the ankle?

Sasha *(finds another pen and writes)*

Not funny.

Narrator: *Uhh Huu*

Wilbert

I grabbed it cause it was kinda different. Then it looked kinda creepy. Now that I look at it, tacky is a more appropriate word. I hoped it would get better but shoot…. It's big enough to fit the kitchen sink.

Sasha *(writes)*

Wha U 2 have with sinks?

Wilbert

Is she serious?

Sizzli *(extending her hand to shake his)*

Yeah! When I first met her, I said the same thing. She said it's in her other bag. Scary isn't it? My name is Sizzli, Sizzli Swinton. This is my… I guess …sister, Sasha.

Wilbert

You guess? Are you related or aren't you?

Danna Dain *(rushing to make sure they didn't break down the salad/pasta bar)*

Is everybody alright? *(pointing at Sasha)* Is she always like that?

Sizzli *(looking shocked)*

Ganna? What are you doing here?

Danna Dain

I work here. And it's Danna! Danna Dain!

Sizzli

Ok whatever. You sure you're not Ganna Gain?

Danna Dain

Do I look like Ganna Gain?

Narrator: *Let's see some ID.*

Sizzli

Well actually-YES! She's my best friend in the whole wide world.

Danna Dain *(striking a pose)*

Well she must be as fiiine as ever.

Sizzli

You **must** be related. She'd say the exact same thing. Amazing! *(pointing at Sasha)* Her? Well, it's a long story I'll give you the condensed version.

First she's a spoiled pain in the – rusty dusty. Then she's my sister and I don't like her. Then we get to Aruba. Yau'll don't like her! Then she's a clutz, then she's speechless, then she's a kite. Then - here we both are.

Narrator: *You could say that! Sasha kite! That was classic.*

Sizzli (cont.)

...we saw this place, I stopped, she landed, we came in, she saw him with that really really tacky bag. Now - she's an idiot. Let's see, did I leave anything out?

Narrator: *Nope. I think that just about covers it.*

Dana Dain

Related? You don't look anything alike. Did I hear you say Sasha Swinton is your sister?

Sizzli

Oh come on!!! Give me a break!!! Please don't tell me that I have to run again.

Danna Dain

Oh no! The Strangest Thing - Ah chew *(she sneezed)* said you have a few minutes to get yourselves together. I've heard the name Sasha Swinton. Maybe from the locals.

What she really needs is to get her self all cleaned up. That'll make her feel better. There's a shower in the back. Got fresh towels and everything. *(Looking at Sasha)* Go on messy, I mean missy, wash some of that stuff off. Quickly! You look like you're from another planet.

Narrator: *That's probably appropriate under the circumstances. Sasha and her handy dandy bag with two hands make their way to* the shower. *Sasha trying to whistle but the only thing coming out of her mouth is wind. It still blows.*

Wilbert *(looking at Danna Dain)*

Did you mean to say, the strangest thing is?

Sizzli

No she meant, the Strangest Thing said. *(looking at Danna and shaking her head)* This is really creepy. Yes we are sisters. You've heard the name? Please enlighten me. What did she do to Aruba?

Danna Dain

I know what I know. Yesh! I heard about her but I'm not one to gossip so you won't hear it from me.

Wilbert

I heard too. And I don't consider it gossiping; I consider it the gathering of information, which can be released at my discretion. It's said that Sasha Swinton, a very spoiled woman, not the brightest bulb in the house, inherited a fortune supposedly from her mother, which made it worse. She's now a very spoiled, very **wealthy** woman. She insisted on having everything personally made and delivered. Real show off to put it mildly. Everything top flight.

Narrator: Did he say flight?

Wilbert *(cont.)*

The only thing that she couldn't have made was a husband so she found a psychic to make a potion for her to find true love. Well her reputation of being both stingy and rather selfish and not really having a clue preceded her so the potion hooked her up with Teddy Toast who took her for everything she had and ran off. Front page news. Something to do with bread. Left her totally and completely broke.

Her credit was no good and her attitude was like an Indian burn. The Arubians had had enough. They put her out of the country and made it clear that she was no longer welcome hence the painting on the sign. Tell tail she doesn't think anybody knows what happened to her money. Personally, I believe she's in denial about it. Sad really.

Sizzli

You've got to be kidding. It was in the News? She does read. That must have been embarrassing, humiliating, un called for, un civilized, and all around not nice.

I, myself, used to lead a very average life. I lived in an apartment big enough for me to cop a squat, one best friend in the whole wide world, *(who looks a lot like Danna - Danna Dain)* and two jobs. One at Handy Dandy Diggs and my second at a place called The Others was my favorite.

My job at The Others, others on my note, Sasha's note, you guys note, *(she looks in the air)* The Strangest Thing and the Palace. OK thing!

Narrator: *Wilbert's eyes got as wide as saucers*

Wilbert

The Strangest Thing? Now there **you** go. My friend was supposed to introduce me to him – it – whatever. *(then he remembers)* The Palace! Waite, I have a note: so he pulls it out of his pocket and shows it to Sizzli.

Sizzli *(reading out loud)*

Responsibilities shift, a change will soon come,
You have traveled the world, but there's work to done.
Look for the others. Not just one party but three,
You'll see that it's more than the place to be. A Palace awaits

Oh snap!!! I got a similar note just before I ran into this crazy lady. Let me see your left shoulder!

Wilbert:

My left WHAT????

Sizzli

Your left shoulder fool. You said you picked up a note. Was it under a medallion and when you tried to pick it up, it shattered but the pieces vanished didn't it? *(she pulled her sleeve over her left shoulder and turned it so he could see the R/S)* Did it have something like this on it? Trust me, the symbol should have moved to your left shoulder. Makes a pretty cool tatoo don't ya think? **Let me see!!**

Wilbert

I will not. So you're telling me that I have been branded. I might not like my last name- Knubbins. Can you believe that? Knubbins. What does that go with? What'd I do?

Narrator: *He's whitty with a charming personality.*

Wilbert (cont.)

I'm whitty with a charming personality.

Narrator: *Told ya*

Danna Dain *(looking at them both)*

Hey! I hate to break up this touching moment but you had a few minutes. That's why I don't gossip, it takes too long. Times up!! There's an exit by the shower room. You can get out that way. I'd suggest you get ghost - toastie!!!!

Sizzli *(looking at Danna and thinking)*

*This really **is** kinda creepy.*

Narrator: *Sizzli goes to the front door and looks down the street. To the right sees a really pissed off Dunno along with Whatabout & Knot. To the left were three more she didn't know at all. One was really Big, one really Tall and the other's looking MEEEEN with her hands balled up heading right for them. Flash lights and everything. Wait a minute, those aren't flash lights.*

Sizzli *(yelling)*

Let's move. Wilbert, you grab little fingies there and I'll get Sasha. *(running down the hall)* Sasha, Sasha! I may not hear you but you can hear me. Gotta go! I mean now! Thanks Ganna! – Danna! Whatever.

Wilbert

Don't tell me! Three Guys!

Sizzli

RRRRRight!! Problem is from which direction? The three to the left I know, the three to the right I have no clue. One's really tall though.

Narrator: *The arms are loose. They run toward the shower room and Wilbert reaches for the bag. First it slaps at his hand. A confused Wilbert has to stop and really get a grip. Really. Sizzli grabs Sasha's hand and out towards the back door they go. Do you see a bell? NO? There good!*

Wilbert

I know those three. They're Guys two brothers and his sister. I'll bet they saw the building lights. Which was probably the only thing that got their attention. *(looking at the bag)* Here I am a grown man, fighting with a tacky bag. I don't believe this. OK, which way do we go?

Narrator: *Well what do you know? The bag with two hands pulled on Wilbert's shirt and pointed towards the docs.*

Wilbert

WHAAA DAAA? *(then looking at Sizzli)* Does this happen in your world often?

Narrator: *Welcome to the family dude.*

Sizzli *(looking at the bag - amazed)*

Just recently. It's pointing towards the water. Let's go! Sorry Sash! I'm not carrying you now either.

Sasha *(squiting her eyes)*

Ahh Nahh!! NOT AGAIN!!!! There's got to be aspirin somewhere in this bag.

Sizzli

I hope you're in good shape fella.

Wilbert

I'm an athlete. With a big tacky bag in my arms. I'll be fine.

Narrator: *The asprin's probably next to the kitchen sink. So we'll try this again. They go toward the door. Well, looks like the plan is coming together. Aren't reunions wonderful? No bell.... OH SNAP! Low Bridge. OOHH SHOOOOT!! Sorry Sasha. We'll have to find you some aspirin.*

Swintons go to Aruba

R/S

Scene VIII

THE GANGS ALL HERE

Scene: Lytl Guy and Wilhoit have gotten to the other side, where the docs are. Along the boarders of the docs, are lots of banners for War On The Water and lots of boats vying for a good position. In first position was Lytl Guy's with the retractable sail and purrs like a kitten. Actually, Tuff pushed the entire set of ships, flags, staffs and everything, down one birth and pulled R/S *ship into place.*

At the gate stood Mr. Clue. He just moved into town not that long ago. Being a pretty good boats man himself, he's keeping an eye on Lytl Guy. Actually, he's been a big help with those little details for the ship. It was, after all, really impressive with the letters R/S *painted on the mast.*

The fellas are boarding at long last.

Narrator: *Where the docs are…someone waits for me. OK maybe not me per say.*

Lytl Guy

Heeey Mr. C, I'm glad ta see you could be here. Um hum You remember Hoity?

Wilhoit

Hey there, Mr. C. How's it hangin'?

Mr. Clue

Well hello young sirs. Looks like it's hangin' just fine. Wanted to check the deetals to make sure everything's in it's place. The barges are ready to be toated and bails are ready to be lifted. Ha Get it? "Toat that barge, lift that bail." Ha ha

Narrator: OK – He thought it was funny. Everybody's trying to be a comedian.

Lytl Guy *(interrupting)*

Thank you Mr. C. I don't think I could have done it without your help. I don't know what brought you to Aruba in the first place but you sure do know a lot about boats. Um Hm

Mr. Clue

Oh young sir, I just know a little of this and a little of that. Feel like I'm in the right place at the right time. This was a really nice birthday present. You've done a great job with the upgrades young sir. I see you're teams a little short a couple people. Isn't it a mandatory 4 people rule? I guess you never know, the strangest thing – Ah chew (he sneezed) could happen.

Wilhoit *(excited)*

Bless you. Is he here? The Strangest Thing? – Ah chew (he sneezed)
Is he here? *(looking at Lytl Guy)* See I told you.

Lytl Guy

Bless the both of you. If there is such a thing, I hope he can sail.
Let's hope your boy Wilbert realizes that you have no way of
competing without a good ship. Um hum If it gets right down to
it, I can use you and Mr. C, and this strangest thing as my crew.
(slapping his head) Oh boy. Come on let's see if I have anything
for that sneezing. Um hum You're making a mess on my boat.

Wilhoit *(waiving)*

Nice seeing you Mr. C.

Guy, I'm telling you, I don't really think it's build for sailing.

Lytl Guy

Whatever!

Mr. Clue. *(looking at Lytl Guy)*

OK young sirs. I think you're ready. You know this course well.
I believe you should be expecting company any minute. One
never know do one? Far be it for me to hold you up. Makes
people frustrated. I'm not good at watching people get frustrated.
Their faces change, speak in languages that I'd never understand
anyway. And…..

Lytl Guy (*interrupts*)

Wish me luck Mr. C. *(and he turns to board)* I just love it when he calls me young sir. I think he must have had a really cranky boss before. Um hum. What is this thing with the Strangest Thing? I don't know what's goin on but let's see if we can find it – him – whatever. This is turning out to be a day that we may never forget. Um hum

Narrator: Unlike the days at Mr. Ruffin's pond which I'm sure he'd would love to forget. The two get on board, check the lines and all the bells and whistles to make sure that everything is set. Then go to the cockpit to check the cranks and knobs and of course the retracting sail. They've got a few minutes or…maybe not. Timing is everything.

Wilhoit *(Looking around this really nice floating machine)*

This is a cool piece of floating apparati. WAAAY better than Willy and mine. What's up with the R/S? Have you picked out a name? This is not just a boat, it's a ship. All Capitaans name their ships.

Lytl Guy

Thanks Hoity. I wanted something that reeks of Royalty. Then Mr. C suggested that, the attraction is the retractable sail. So I figured simply R/S. It's sounds regal but has a hidden meaning. Um hum.

Narrator: Could this be coincidence? Destiny maybe? Looks like just due in the making.

Wilhoit

Well you're a painindabutt. Why don't you name her The Royal PIB. Ha ha!

Lytl Guy

Oh you're funny. This has always been my really intense pleasure. But I think I'll keep it just the way it is. Um hum,

Narrator: *Yeah cause RIP could be misunderstood.*

Wilhoit

What do you mean always been? You've only had it for two years. I remember when your father got it for you. First the deck wasn't wide enough. Then the colors for the mast weren't right, then the sails didn't retract fast enough. Then the bathroom towels didn't match the walls. Then.....

Lytl Guy

Alright. Alright. It may not have been prefect, it took a lot of overpriced work but now that it's complete, you keep talking about this strangest thing, wouldn't it be the strangest thing if after we start WOW I'd just ....

(Looking at the clock) It'll be starting in a few hours. I hate saying this, and don't you ever repeat it, but I know I can't win this without the best team working with me. Um hum It won't work with my family. Bunch of door knobs.

Narrator: *That's acceptance.*

Wilhoit *(interrupts)*

I was gonna mention that....

Lytl Guy

I've seen you and Willy work. Um hum. If you can pull a win like the one last year by using that piece of...

Wilhoit

Watch it!!!

Lytl Guy

You know what I mean. Together we could be unstoppable. Plus I showed you the note...... Look for the others. Um hum

Narrator: Looks like the others are headed right for them.

> **Scene: Running up the docs towards the boat, Lytl Guy sees three people. Two were running like maniacs whose lives depended getting away from something quickly and the strangest flying apparatus he'd ever seen hanging on for dear life. And some man with this huge tacky bag with bizarre handles, that looks like he should really give it back.**

Lytl Guy

Hoity! You see what I see? Um hum

Narrator: It's a bird. It's a plane. IIIIt's Sssasha Kiiiite and her handy yet tacky sidekick Little Fingies.....

Wilhoit

Hey, that's Wilbert. What's he running for? Who are those ladies and why is one in the air?

Sizzli

Special delivery!!! All aboard people!!! Whatever!! Get out of the way!!!! **MOVE**!!!

Wilbert

Move it or loose it!!!!

Sasha *(looking down at the dock)*

Nice ship.......Is that **MY DRIVER** down there? MAN? What is his name?

Narrator: *Here she comes. She's coming, cooming, looower, loooower. Nice way to work that line. Impressive! Sizzli's getting good at this. Sasha still can't land on her feet. Ouch! Sheeez down. Sheez up. Shez good.*

Mr. Clue. *(tilting his head)*

Good day ma ladies.

Narrator: Sasha hears the voice and turns around to see Mr. Clue, who bears an uncanny resemblance to Mr. D her old driver. You should see her grabbing at Mr. Clue yelling in languages that he probably wouldn't appreciate but definitely can't hear anyway.

They make eye contact and from the expression he saw on her face and the way her hair was standing on end and fire around her head... good ol Mr. C takes off running to his Benz which is parked waaaaay at the other end of the docs. He gets in and squeals out the parking area, into the sunset.

Sasha *(realizes)*

That's my driver. Man! Man! What is his name?

Narrator: *Wilbert dropped the bag and it got an attitude. Jus' what you need, a bag with an attitude. It could lock fingers never to be opened again. Humpf*

Sizzli *(trying to catch her breath, grabs one of little fingies hands and smacks Sasha on the calf.)*

Sasha, stop that! Leave that man alone. *(looking around)* Hey party people. Nice boat. Mind if we keep you company for a minute? HMMMMM?

Wilhoit

Hey Wilbert. Where'd you go? I turned around and you were gone. Diiiid Guy huuurt your feeeelings?

Narrator: *It ended up having something to do with veg-e-tables.*

Wilbert

No. Big, Tall and Tuff. I ran into 'em after you left me – wherever. I hooked a right and I guess they tracked me down. They caught up to me – us at The Plaace 2 B. No offense Guy but your people are dumb as door knobs!!!

Wilhoit

I was gonna mention that.

Sizzli

Oh that's who they were. Big, Tall and Tuff? I'da never guessed by the looks of things. They were coming from the left. I saw Dunno, Whatabout and Knot from - It. - the mall coming from the right. Sasha sorta shed sand allll over their property and when Dunno recognized her, we had to make a hasty retreat. And didn't pay for our sandwiches.

Narrator: Yeah but you got your just dew for free.

Wilbert

Big & Tall are Lytl's brothers from another mother and Tuff's his sister – those Guys *(looking at Lytl)* How did you know that I found a note?

Lytl Guy

(looking at Sasha) He's right. Those "Guys" are my stepsister Tuff and my two other brothers Big and Tall. *(Looking at Wilbert)* What did you mean, how did I know you found a note? **IIII** found a note. A medallion and a note, like I told you. *(so he reached for the note to show it to Wilbert but it wasn't there.)* Where'd it go??

Wilhoit *(looking at Wilbert)*

You found a note too? The Strangest Thing (ah chew) didn't make mention of that little detail. *(looking in the air)*You got jokes too. Baaad Thing. Bad. Bad

Narrator: *Yeah but it is kinda funny.*

Wilbert

Hoity, I found it this morning. You were right there and weren't looking so I grabbed it.

Lytl Guy *(extending his hand to Sizzli)*

My name is Lytl. Lytl Guy. The finest sailor in allll of Aruba. And who might you be fine lady? With you on board, my nautical beauty, I can beat any boat in any water at any time. Welcome aboard. Yes you aaarrre a special deeelivery. Wilbert, introduce me to your friends.

Wilhoit *(extending his hand to Sasha)*

Well hi there ahhh lady. Do you know you have sand all over you? Hey! Have I seen you before? Yeah. I know you!

Sizzli *(trying to catch her breath)*

Alright! Go 'head on! Take her! Shoot! I'm not running another step and my arms hurt. I don't like her anyway - either.

Wilbert *(putting his arm on Sizzli's shoulder)*

Let me introduce you. This is Sizzli Swinton and her sister Sasha. Look here you height challenged.... Step awaaay from the lady. You can just barely look above her belly button.

I met them by the salad/pasta bar at The Plaace 2 B. Trust me, she doesn't want you.

Wilhoit

I knew it. I knew it. Sasha Swinton, You're not even supposed to be here in Aruba. You must not read good do ya?

Narrator: *Not to hear her tell it.*

Lytl Guy *(looking at Sizzli)*

Well nobody will see you here. I'll make sure of that. *(Moving closer to Sizzli)* The Guy Team. Um hum!

Wilbert *(stepping between them)*

Nobody will see you over the steering wheel. Just caus you're short on body doesn't make you short of hearing. She don't want chew!!!

Sizzli *(rolling her eyes)*

Please believe. I need a drink. Can I get a nice cold glass of prune juice on the rocks and smalteen crakers?

Narrator: *Put it in a little glass. Come on, he's got a set with "L/G". Lytl Guy? Little glass? Whatever.*

Lytl Guy

You're in luck. I just so happened to have a 24 pack of prune juice and smalteen crackers in the cupboard. Prune juice and smalteen crachers. It's the bestest snack in the eeentire world. Mmm mmm mmm mmm yummy. Never sail without them.

Narrator: *Are they related or what?*

Wilhoit

What do you mean salad/pasta bar at The Plaace 2 B? There's no such place.

Sizzli

Oh yes there is.

Narrator: *Gotta admit it was a great view especially from Sasha's angle.*

Sizzli *(cont.)*

Sasha got her roll on, made a mess, we got busted, didn't know which way to go, ran inside The Plaace 2 B, were being followed, the bag pointed us this way so here we are.

Guy, you found a note too. Wilbert, let me see your note again. *(He took it out of his pocket.) It read:*

Want to travel the world but you don't really know.
You're looking for something, so which way do you go.
You'll see that it's more than the place to be.
The others are looking. Not one party but three,

A Palace awaits.

Lytl Guy

I memorized mine. It said:

Responsibilities shift, a change will soon come,
You have traveled the world but there's work to done.
Look for the others. Not just one party but three,
You'll see that it's more than the place to be.

A Palace awaits.

Sizzli

So you see fellas, the note told you not one party but three. *(looking at Wilhoit)* You've met Sasha and I, and it looks like Guy makes three.

Narrator: *Over the microphone there was the voice saying.*

Voice:

Ladies and Gentleman!

Welcome to the 27ᵗʰ Annual
WAR ON THE WATER.
We've got perfect weather for a perfect race.

START YOUR ENGINES!!

Guy *(looking as Sizzli)*

Alright, besides flying a mean kite, do you know anything about sailing? You think you can run the lines?

Sizzli

Well I did use to live on grandpa's boat in the summer. We would race for corn.

Wilbert

Oh shucks

Narrator: *I was thinking the same thing.*

Sizzli *(pointing her finger)*

Yea yea yea shucks. Where have I heard that one before? So original. Now. I don't know about Sasha. If you ask her, she'll probably say she had somebody do the sailing for her allllll the way from - wherever.

Sasha *(writing another note)*

How'd U know?

Lytl Guy *(looking at Sasha)*

Look, you stay there and duck when I tell you to. Well before we start, *(getting closer to Sizzli)* lets huddle up.

Sizzli

Waite! I've got to tell you something. Remember that medallion with that crest that shattered when you picked it up that looks like the one coincidently on the mast.

Wilbert and Lytl

Yeah!

Sizzli

Well, I need to see your left shoulder. That's how we'll know that you are a Swinton!

Narrator: Let's see! Come on. Take off those shirts. Don't be embarrassed.

Sasha *(rubbing her forehead and writing another note)*

I've got a head ach.

Lytl Guy

I'll show you later. Huddle up.

*Narrator: That's all they needed to get this party started--- **right**. You know what a huddle looks like. Seems like a human "O" to me.*

Voice:

ON YOUR MARKS....GET SET...

Narrator: We're on this really big Royal ship (R/S). Wilbert and Lytl Guy have just met these ladies but they'll just have to stay put and hope for the best. This is the War on The Water. What an exciting event. Who could ask for anything moooore.

So now the fellas have just received some life changing information about a medallion and notes that they both found and the prospect that their future has changed. Sizzli was filling them in on what it meant just before the huddle. Looked like a human "O" to me. What do you think? What would happen if we huddle and someone doesn't have R/S?

Swintons go to Aruba

R/S

Scene IX

INCLUDES SHIPPING AND HANDLING

Scene: Everyone has been introduced. Looks like Lytl Guy has his dream team. He said that he couldn't do this without Wilbert, well now he has Sasha and Sizzli too. He doesn't know the women but he will soon. Sasha may be getting finger cramps from writing since she still has no voice. Actually, now she does but she doesn't know that yet either. Won't they be surprised?

There are those times when you hope for the best. There are those times when you just want your just due. Their lives will never be the same. This could be a good thing. They'll win the race of a lifetime. *THREE – TWO - ONE – BREAK!!*

Narrator: *They break from the huddle and are in different surroundings but they haven't noticed yet. The water's a little bluer, a little calmer…*

Lytl Guy *(grabbing Sizzli's hand)*

Now what's that you were saying about a palace? I don't know about all that but as long as it's with you darlin'…

Sizzli

Guy! Your grippin' me. Stop reaching. I'm not picking you up.

Wilbert

Man. Take your tiny hands off her. This could be your sister and she don't want you. Even if you were full grown!

Lytl Guy *(balling up his fist)*

I'll show you full grown!

Narrator: *Oh sibling rivalry. Don't you just love it?*

Sizzli

Look fellas, Let me explain. We are Swintons. Royal Swintons, no less. Like I was telling Wilbert. Sasha and I both found a medallion and a note saying "A Palace awaits". So I'm here to tell you that a Palace is waiting for both of you - too.

Lytl Guy

I must say that sounds interesting. Um hum. I knew it. Mr. C was always saying that he was givng me the royal treatment and I should get used to it. Strange man really. He just came from out of nowhere. All I know is that if it weren't for him...He helped me with the palette and design of this ship and it felt right when I put those letters and colors on the mast. It's really is regal huh?

Narrator: *Check out little fingies. It's giving the thumbs up. It's thumbs are sooo little. No offense Guy.*

Sizzli

It's more like Royal. You see, when Sasha and I met, we were both told about something called The Strangest Thing. We met him, at the Palace. He told us that we were not only sisters but part of a huge International Royal family. We were sent to find you and bring you to the palace. I think the huddle may have helped with that part. I'll bet you didn't know that you had an inheritance did ya?

Narrator: *Wilbert, you can't sing now either.*

Lytl Guy

You've got to be joking! A palace?

Sasha (*Looking at Lytl Guy wrote*)

No joke. Das means we keep the boat. Humpf!

Lytl Guy (*looking around*)

Waite a minute! Where are the rest of the boats? Did we get that far ahead that fast? Man I'm good!

Wilbert

Are you serious? No you're not good. You're probably lost. I knew that I shouldn't be sailing with you. Ugg! None of this looks familiar. You did it this time half pint. You should have made a left turn at Malbuquerqee. This is the strangest thing.

Narrator: *Appearing, as if out of no where is the hostest with* *the mostest, "**The Strangest Thing**". (I had to do that for effect.)*

Imagine the shock from the fellahs when they see that it is in fact the strangest thing they've ever seen. A pogo stick. It's true that looks can be deceiving. Don't judge a book buy it's cover and …..

The Strangest Thing

Well Wilbert, thanks for the introduction. No fellahs, you're not lost. You're home.

Narrator: *The other ships weren't invited.*

The Strangest Thing (cont.)

See here's the thing. **I** am the Strangest Thing. The fact that you're here proves that you've heard of me.

Wilbert

Sizzli, you got some splainin' to do.

Sasha *(pulled out a felt tip looking really mad wrote)*

YES U D ꝋꝋ

Narrator : *I guess the pen ran out.*

Lytl Guy *(rubbing his eyes)*

You've got to be kidding. You're a stick - thingy. And you talk. What???

Narrator: *Yeah, and you're Lytl.*

Sizzli

Gentleman, let me introduce you to my fathers creation. This is what we've been talking about. This is indeed The Strangest Thing.

Wilbert

Yeah right. Your father's creation? He couldn't think of anything else to use to send a message. Wespill Onion? Fend Ax? A courier pigeon? Noooo A pogo stick!

Narrator: *Don't be mad!*

The Strangest Thing

I'm not going to take any of that personally. You see, here's the thing - Your parents are triplets. Two boys and one girl. Because of a family dispute they separated. Moved to different parts of the world with no forwarding address or anything.

After years of misery with the left hand not knowing what the right hand is doing, Sizzli's father created me. He made me to be a combination of the strength of metal; to keep the family strong when they're together. Handles; to make sure you get a grip and a pogo stick body since your family's attitudes bounce up and down.- it seemed appropriate

Sasha

But wait there's more.

Lytl Guy

More. I'm still trying to figure out where the other boats are. What I see is a stick….. What more could there be?

Narrator: *Who could ask for anyting mooooooore?*

The Strangest Thing

Here's the thing, it's the narrow wings down bottom. I'm not sure what they're for. *(turning to the side and back)* I still think they make me look too skinny. Anyway, here's the thing, his next thing was to bring the family together. But how you may ask? Glad you ask. He and a friend, made the medallions with R/S in the middle. As you have seen, when you touch it, it shatters…… Only a Swinton can do that too.

Sizzli (interrupts)

…. you get a great tatoo Nice isn't it?

Strangest Thing (cont.)

That's the identifier. There are a lots of Swintons but not all Royal. Everybody with a cold hasn't seen me. When a Royal Swinton touches the left shoulder with the right hand, that get's you connected to each other. And I, Me, The Strangest Thing happens.

Sizzli

Make sort of a human O, it's supposed to be for "Others", and you get connected. Better than AD&D. That's what we did when he made that huddle. Looks to me like we're all related, *(looking at Lytl Guy)* so little dude, you need to keep your hands to yourself.

Sasha *(got another piece of paper)*

Wilbert? No way. Lytl Guy? Jus luv the ship. You're my brother 2? *(pumping her fist and mouthing)* Whoo Hoo!

The Strangest Thing

Sasha, honey. You have a voice so you can stop writing now.

Sizzli

Shame!

Sasha *(excited and stretching her hand from writing)*

I can talk again. Woo hoo! Did you see what this girl did to me? Humpf! She laughed at me when I fell allll the way down that sandy beach. Paraded me around in public with me looking a mess and gave me a head ach. – Twice. I think she did it on purpose by pulling me through the air. That wasn't funny. *(the view was lovely though)* Humpf. **DO SOMETHING!** It was embarrassing, humiliating, un called for, un civilized, and over all not nice ...humpf!

Can't we take her fortune away?

Narrator: *You said you loved to fly. OK so you didn't get peanuts. You fit in with out fitting in – exactly. The Sasha kite was a keeper.*

Sizzli

Well, you were flying in that limo, I just took it to another level. MORON! Believe it or not sis, I was saving your life. And I don't even like you. I told you Arubians don't like you. I don't like you either but I'm stuck with you and did I tell you that I don't like you?

Sasha

I don't care! Yoooooou were the one that didn't hear the sneeze plus - gave a headach – **TWICE!! Humpf!**

Sizzli

We were on a hill Sasha. And you don't do walking. You roll and you fly- that's it. Like I said isn't gravity just grand?

Narrator: Gotta love it.

The Strangest Thing

Sizzli, I must commend you on your quick wit and gift of improvisation. What you did at the restaurant was terrific. You're just like your father. He can always make something happen.

Sizzli *(looking at Sasha)*

You have to admit Sash, it was kinda of fun.

Sasha

Fun schmun! Like I said, you gave me a head ach. HUMPF!!!

Sizzli

Now you know how I feel when you talk so much alllll the time, alllll the time. *Alright, I could have ask you to duck. OOPPS!!*

Narrator: *I didn't say that. Now comes the Q & A. The Strangest Thing has to fill the fellahs in on how their lives have changed.*

The Strangest Thing *(turning towards Sasha)*

We'll take care of the head ach but you got an opportunity that nobody else has.

Narrator: *Yeah, the best view imaginable.*

Sizzli

Tell me something? Was that my friend Ganna at The Plaace 2 B or a twin?

The Strangest Thing

I'm glad you ask. Here's the thing. I couldn't really leave you out there by yourselves especially for the first time out. Thought you may need help sometimes. Remember when I told you that a friend of the Swinton will be the only one to see me? Well they have been chosen just like you to follow you on your travels, keep you out of trouble and direct you when you need it. The Plaace 2 B was a decoy and no it didn't really exist. And if you'll notice, you just transpose the L and A and you have Palace.

Wilhoit

You're just a crafty thing aren't you?

Narrator: *Whatever works!*

Lytl Guy

No wonder I've never heard of it. Aren't you just the clever one?

Sasha

Yeah so that **was** my driver wasn't it? *What was his name?* Humpf! When I see him again, I'm want my car. It was a Benz. I got it for my birthday sent to me all the way back from....

Narrator: *Sasha they won't remember you.*

The Strangest Thing

OK Sasha. I know. They have a mission just like you. So when you move, they move.

Narrator: *Just like that.*

The Strangest Thing (cont.)

Now fellas, let the ladies see your left shoulder.

Narrator: *You heard the stick - thing. Don't be shy now. There you have it, on their left shoulder is, in fact the R/S.*

Sizzli

See, I told you. You are family.

Lytl Guy

I see. So who were my parents and how did they fit into this whole thing? Does this mean that I'll have to change my name to Lytl Swinton? Can't I just be L.

Narrator: *What? This is not a secret alien agency?*

Sasha

Wouldn't you rather be called Mr. Swinton. That's better don't you think?

Lytl Guy

Well, yeah! That sounds great. Mr. Swinton. I like it. Better than Mr. Guy.

Wilbert

Well now isn't that just special. I know that I was adopted and from what I've heard so is this Guy. Who are our parents and why did they give us up for adoption?

The Strangest Thing

Well, here's the thing, Your mother – Wanda, was one of a set of triplets There were two boys and a girl. Sasha and Sizzli have the same father – William. And Lytl's father - Wayne.

Because they fell out, neither of your parents knew that there was a palace waiting and due to circumstances beyond their control, they couldn't afford to keep you so they sent you to somebody who would take good care of you. It took me a while to find you so when I did, I sent the medallion.

Anyway, here's the thing, if you remember the notes all say – find the others. Now this is your job.

Narrator: *And you have no choice but to accept it.*

The Strangest Thing (cont.)

The ladies found you and you're not the only ones out there so we're just getting started. Come into the palace and I'll show you around and explain where you go from here.

Wilbert

Tell me something. I noticed that every time somebody says your name they sneeze. What is that about?

Sizzli

My father kept a cold so when he sneezed "that one" told him that it looked like the strangest thing so that's what he named it – The Strangest Thing. OK he definately had jokes.

Since he's a blessing when the right person says it's name, they sneeze, you say bless you, and you know what happens next so.....

Lytl Guy or should I say Mr. Swinton

I guess I can accept that. I did have a pretty good life. I can't complain I mean look at this boat. But this is soooo much better than anything that I'd ever imagined. We have family all over and now are we supposed to travel all the way around the world to find relatives that we don't even know?

Sasha

Allll the way around the world. Allll the way. Humpf

Wilbert

My life was crap. I stayed back in the fourth grade four times and the only thing I ever got was a hard way to go. **WHY KNUBINS???** I hate that name. It doesn't go with any thing.

The Strangest Thing

Your mother, Wanda did that. OOPPPSS!!

Narrator: *She thought it was funny. I wonder if she could sing?*

Wilbert

(looks in the air) Thanks MOM!! So how on earth are we supposed to travel to find anybody? Me and my mother need to talk.

The Strangest Thing

Here's the thing. To move around, make a huddle like you did to get here, put me in the middle, get a grip, pound me on the ground two times and just say anywhere and you're there. But once you lose your grip, I'm gone. You will not see me again until you find your family and come back to the palace.

The Swinton will find you. They will have been told about The Strangest Thing, found the medallion, which will have transferred the R/S to their left shoulders. Once they've found you, huddle up and you will be right here at the Palace.

Sasha

Just don't get carried away with the pounding.

Narrator: He's not getting any younger ya know.

Lytl Guy

But we're on a boat. This doesn't look like a palace to me.

The Strangest Thing

Look to your left. You'll see the palace. This is the lake behind the palace. I had it built myself. Pretty nifty if I do say so myself. I knew it would come in handy.

Narrator: Don't say that too loud, you may offend the bag.

The Strangest Thing (cont.)

Well here's the thing, the ladies already know how it works. Did the women tell you that your family didn't really get along? Because the family needed love, the R/S was the key. All they really needed was a hug.

Narrator: I think I'm gonna cry.

Sasha

You must not have heard me, I HAVE A HEADACH!!!! Humpf! *(looking at Guy)* Little person, go fetch me an aspirin! NOW!!!! Humpf!

Little Guy

Listen here lady. You don't know me. You just met me. I'll tell you where you can go.

Narrator: *To find the aspirin right?*

Wilbert

Yeah, if I'm not mistaken, you'll find aspirin allllll the way down the hall....

Sizzli

And you can have one delivered personally alllll the way to your mouth by your fingers or will that offend your bag.

The Strangest Thing

Well, I'm sure you want to see your new home. Here's the thing, if you all would give each other a hug, put me in the middle, get a grip with the left hand bounce me twice and let me do the rest. Your palace awaits!

Sasha

A hug! Yeah right! **Can I PAA LEEEEASE** get an aspirin?

Sizzli *(completely amazed)*

Woa! Take note fellas, Sasha said Please! What an accomplishment!

Narrator: *Now can I do the daa daa daaaa part? Sasha and Siz-*

zli have gone into International waters. Well there in water at least. So here we are. This would be a great opportunity for Sasha to take a pill and wash the sand off. Fortunately, she's left Aruba with her functioning parts still functioning, plus or minus one.......

Then you find two fellas who didn't really like each other in the first place but will have to grin and bear it or maybe even move to a different part of the palace. Is this what happens when you find out that you aren't who you thought you were?

You have to admit it sounded like fun didn't it? Again I ask, isn't the family dynamic a wonderful thing?

Which will come first?

Impression? Intention? Payback? Or Just due?

Looks like all these things came one at a time. As you see, every story has a heroin and hero with their trusty sidekick to keep them out of trouble. Isn't it great how these folks can run and talk at the same time? Ain't multitasking a wonderful thing?

So far, two more Swinton's have been added to the party and that's not the only thing that's been added - a ship. Woo Huu.

But wait, there's more. We aren't done yet but you knew that part didn't you? Want to pick up the next book don't you? I would. But it's my job. Somebody's got to do it.

Soooo...... There you have it. Ya'll come back now ha hear!!!